D1120297

The hedgehog bridegroom was joyful. His new young wife was timid. "I'm not sleepy yet," she said to the hedgehog boy.

So the hedgehog boy went to bed by himself. Stepping out of his clothes, he laid them on the bedspread. Then he took off his coat of fur and hung it on the bedpost. Climbing into bed, he was soon fast asleep.

When the princess at last crept into the bedroom, she was astonished to see her husband's prickly coat hanging on the bedpost.

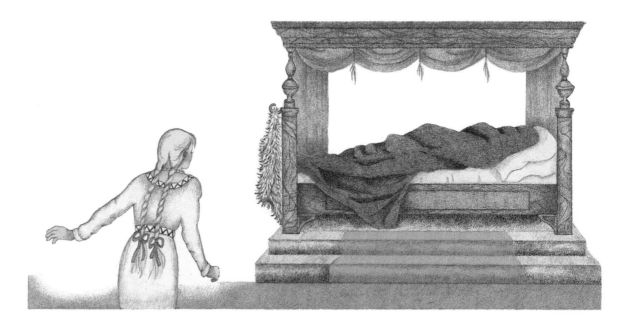

"I like my new husband," she thought, "but I certainly don't like his prickles!" Snatching down the coat of fur from the bedpost, she ran outside and tossed it into a Midsummer bonfire.

At once the fire roared and flamed up as high as the stars. Instantly the hedgehog boy's furry coat was burned to ashes.

Hot and flushed, the princess ran back into the bedroom.

Her bridegroom was sitting up, shivering. "Oh, wife," he said faintly, "I think I am dying!" Then he fell back on the pillow.

"Oh, what have I done?" thought the princess, and she fell on her knees beside the bed.

For many days her husband lay at the point of death.

The princess spent every hour at his bedside. She filled the room with sweet-smelling flowers, and fed him honey from her own beehives, and prayed that the hedgehog boy would live.

But the king stroked his chin, and said to himself, "If he dies, it will be all for the best."

Little by little, the hedgehog boy grew better. At last, on the night of the new moon, he stood up, completely well.

No longer was he a hedgehog boy. He was a good-looking young man!

The princess clapped her hands. Together they rejoiced.

The king, too, was delighted. "I always thought you were a good fellow," he said. "You shall be king after me."

And then there was a celebration, with stuffed goose and sauerkraut, fresh pike and roast pig, and beer flowing freely from the keg. There was dancing and singing, and blowing of horns.

The farmer and his wife were invited to come to the feast, and to live in the castle. They came joyfully, and brought all their pigs.

But in the castle barnyard, the old wife tugged at her husband's sleeve. "Look," she said, "I told you. Scrawny pigs! Ours are fatter. Ours have curlier tails."

And when she saw what had happened to her hedgehog boy, the prickly baby she had found in the basket so long ago, she was prouder still. She nudged her husband with her elbow. "What a handsome young man! Well, what would you expect, with such good-looking parents?"

Then the farmer's wife danced with the king, and bumped into a basket of cabbages, and sat down and laughed.

Only the two older sisters were grumpy. They sat beside their husbands with scowling faces. The prime minister was too fat to dance. The toothless old general could only suck soup from a spoon.

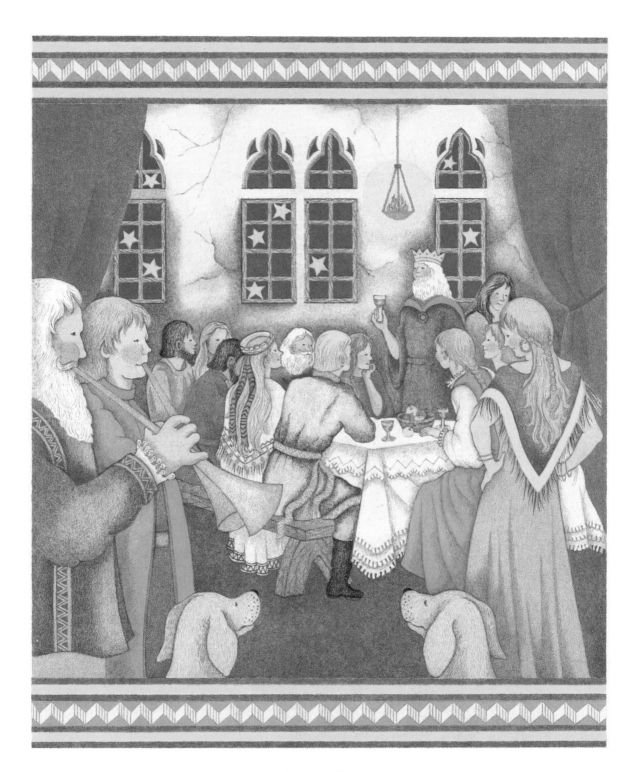

But the youngest princess and her bridegroom danced all night long, till the sun came up and the roosters crowed to greet the morning.

– The End –

KUR TU TECI, GAILĪTI MANU
WHERE ARE YOU GOING, ROOSTER MINE?

Kur tu te - ci, kur tu te - ci, gai - lī - ti manu?
Roo - ster mine, where are you go - ing, shout - ing so loud?

Kur tu te - ci, kur tu te - ci, gai - lī - ti manu?
Roo - ster mine, where are you go - ing, shout - ing so loud?

No rī - ti - i - ņa ag - ru - mā - i
In the ear - ly_____ sum - mer morn, The

No rī - ti - i - ņa ag - ru - mā?
bright and ear - ly_____ sum - mer morn?

2.

Ciemā teku, ciemā teku, meitas celt
Ciemā teku, ciemā teku, meitas celt
No rītiņa agrumā
No rītiņa agrumā

2.

Pretty girls are sleeping in the house next door,
Pretty girls are sleeping in the house next door.
Cock-a-doodle! I must wake them!
Cock-a-doodle! Maids, wake up!

3.

Celies, mana, celies, mana, līgaviņ,
Celies, mana, celies, mana līgaviņ,
Jau gailītis nodziedāja
Jau gailītis nodziedāja!

3.

Wake, my dear one, wake, my dear one, my darling bride!
Wake, my dear one, wake, my dear one, my darling bride!
I have greeted the day for you!
Yes, I have sung my sweet song for you!

(English verses loosely adapted from the Latvian)

THE
HEDGEHOG
BOY

A LATVIAN FOLKTALE

RETOLD BY JANE LANGTON

ILLUSTRATED BY ILSE PLUME

HARPER & ROW, PUBLISHERS

The Hedgehog Boy
Text copyright © 1985 by Jane Langton
Illustrations copyright © 1985 by Ilse Plume
Printed in the U.S.A. All rights reserved.
1 2 3 4 5 6 7 8 9 10
First Edition

Library of Congress Cataloging in Publication Data
Langton, Jane.
    The hedgehog boy.

    Summary: A princess is forced to marry a prickly
hedgehog boy and is astounded when remorse over a
thoughtless act of hers transforms him into a handsome
young man.
    [1. Fairy tales.   2. Folklore—Latvia]   I. Plume, Ilse,
ill. II. Title.
PZ8.L28He 1985   [398.2] [E]   83-47698
ISBN 0-06-023696-5
ISBN 0-06-023697-3 (lib. bdg.)

for
Karen Nelson Hoyle
and
Valerija Bērziņa-Baltiņa

A long time ago, when pretzels still fell from the sky like rain, an old farmer and his wife sat by their doorstep at the edge of the great forest.

"If only we had a son," said the farmer. "Then we would have someone to care for. I would make him a little fur hat. I would teach him to tend the pigs."

"Or a daughter," sighed his wife. "I would braid her hair with a ribbon. She could help me feed the chickens."

But the old man and his wife had only a few squealing pigs, a flock of clucking hens, and a pair of noisy roosters. There were no children laughing and playing around their knees.

One day the farmer took his pigs into the great forest. The pigs ran fast and led him deep into the woods.

To his surprise, he came upon a cottage in a clearing. There sat the Forest Mother, wearing a crown of white clover.

She smiled at him and gave him a basket. "Take it home with you," she said. "Put it behind the stove, and do not open it for three days."

The farmer took the basket. And then, before he could thank her, the Forest Mother disappeared. Her cottage, too, had vanished. The clearing was empty.

Bewildered, the farmer carried the basket home and showed it to his wife.

"What's in it?" she said, bending down to peek under the lid.

"You mustn't look," said the farmer, putting the basket behind the stove. "It's a gift from the Forest Mother."

"But I'm hungry," said his wife. "Maybe it's something to eat— a fine big cheese, or a loaf of bread."

"No, no," said her husband. "Leave it alone. We mustn't open it for three days."

"Well, all right then," said the old woman. Sitting down beside the stove, she watched the basket all day long.

On the first day it trembled.

On the second day it rocked and jiggled.

On the third day, when the farmer and his wife woke up, the basket was making small cooing sounds.

The farmer and his wife jumped out of bed, and the old woman ran to open the lid.

Inside the basket was a baby. But it was not an ordinary baby.

The old woman burst into tears. "Look," she wept, "it's covered with prickles, like a hedgehog!"

But the old man said, "Never mind. It is better to have this child than no child at all."

The years passed quickly—summer, fall, winter, and spring—summer, fall, winter, and spring. Before long the hedgehog baby was a hedgehog boy. He was still covered with stiff fur, but his mind was as sharp as his prickles, and he was cheerful and trustworthy. When he was old enough, his father sent him into the forest to take care of the pigs.

The hedgehog boy tended them well.

Every day he led them to places where the acorns lay thick on the ground.

Every night he made a bonfire to keep them warm, and he sat beside them, playing his whistle.

Every year new pigs were born. The hedgehog boy cared for them tenderly until they were as big and fat as the others. The herd grew larger and larger.

On the other side of the great forest was a town, where the king lived in his castle. The king had three daughters, a pair of fine horses, and a barnyard full of chickens, cows, and pigs.

It was June. All the people of the town were enjoying the festival of Midsummer Eve. Boys and girls made wreaths of oak leaves and flowers. Fathers decked their houses and barns with branches of oak and ash, to inspire their cabbages to grow big and their sheep to have twins. Mothers put fishbones at stable doors to drive away witches. And young girls went to the river to see in the water the faces of the men they would marry.

The king's daughters, too, went to the river, hoping to see the faces of their future husbands.

The eldest princess saw the face of the fat prime minister. She was pleased. The prime minister was rich, with many farms. "Surely," she thought, "he will be king when my father dies."

The middle princess saw the face of the toothless old general, and she was happy too. The general had many men under his command. "He will be the next king after my father," she thought, "and I will be queen."

But the youngest princess saw the face of a strange creature, and she was terrified. It wasn't the face of a man at all. It was the prickly face of a hedgehog!

The frightened princess did not tell her sisters what she had seen. Instead, she mounted her horse and rode alone into the woods.

Among the dark trees, the princess's horse quivered at the rattle of dry leaves under his hooves. Suddenly a rabbit darted across the path. The horse reared and plunged, and galloped away with the princess.

The branches were low and bristling. Sharp twigs tore at her hair. The princess screamed at the horse to stop. But he galloped on.

Luckily the hedgehog boy was nearby, sitting beside the bonfire with his pigs. When he heard the thud of the horse's hooves and the cries of the princess, he ran to meet her, and grabbed the reins of the runaway horse.

At once the horse stood still, panting and tossing his head.

The princess gasped with relief. Jumping down, she cried, "You have saved my life."

But when she saw the prickly face of the hedgehog boy, she was frightened once more. It was the face she had seen in the river!

The hedgehog boy smiled at her. "Come sit by the fire," he said.

But the princess was afraid. "I must go," she said. "My father will wonder what has become of me. I am the youngest daughter of the king."

Climbing back on her horse, she rode quickly away.

But that night, as the Midsummer bonfires blazed in the streets of the town, she couldn't forget the smiling face of the hedgehog boy.

And the hedgehog boy, in his turn, could not forget the flushed cheeks and tangled braids of the princess, and the way she had hopped bravely down among his pigs.

One day, hearing again the jingle of spurs and the thump of a horse's hooves on the forest track, he sprang to his feet.

But it was not the princess. It was her father, the king. He had lost his way in the great forest.

Finding himself among pigs, the king called loudly to the boy who was tending the herd, "Tell me how to find my way home, and I will give you a penny." But then he looked more closely at the hedgehog boy. "And tell me how such a prickly little man can take care of so many pigs!"

The hedgehog boy smiled at the king. "How can such a *big* man lose his way in the forest?" And then he bowed. "Yes, of course I will show you the way home. Only promise me that I may marry your youngest daughter."

"What?" cried the king angrily. "Never!" Turning his horse around, he rode back into the woods, heading in the wrong direction.

The next day the king came back. He had been riding in a circle. He was tired and hungry. "Come, boy, show me the way home," he said, his voice cracking with thirst, "and I will give you a barrel of fish."

Again the hedgehog boy bowed politely. "I will show you the way," he said, "but you must give me the hand of your youngest daughter in marriage."

"Impossible," groaned the king. "How could she marry a pincushion?" And away he went again, into a storm of wind and rain.

Next day the king turned up again in the clearing, limping beside his stumbling horse. His face was muddy. He had slept in a puddle. There were twigs in his hair and a crack in his amber crown. "Help me, hedgehog boy," he whispered hoarsely. "If you will show me the way home, I will give you a farm and a house of logs."

"Of course I will show you the way home," said the hedgehog boy, jumping down from his tree stump. "But I don't want a farm. I want to marry your youngest daughter."

What could the poor king do? He would never find his way home by himself. Gloomily, he picked a splinter out of his thumb. "Well, take her then," he said.

Joyfully, the hedgehog boy led the weary king safely to the edge of the great forest.

"I will come for my bride next Midsummer Eve," he said. "You won't forget your promise?"

"No," said the king, shaking his head ruefully. "A promise is a promise." Then the king dragged himself home.

The king told his youngest daughter to prepare her wedding dress and fill her bridal chest with linens. She was going to be married next Midsummer Eve.

"Married?" cried the princess. "But who will be my husband?"

"Wait and see," said the king gruffly.

Obediently, the princess sat down at her loom. She remembered the prickly face she had seen in the river and the strange young man who had saved her life in the forest.

Was he to be her bridegroom?

In the great forest the year passed slowly. All through the fall and winter and spring, the hedgehog boy stayed in the woods with his pigs. At last he went home to his father and mother, driving the herd before him.

"So many pigs," cried his father. "They will fill the whole barn."

"And such curly tails," cried his mother. "Surely they are the fattest pigs in all the world!"

"I've tended the pigs long enough," said the hedgehog boy. "Now I must go to town to find a wife."

"Oh, be careful," warned his mother. "She will be greedy. She will marry you for your beautiful pigs!"

Nevertheless, his mother patched his trousers and made him a new shirt, and his father made him a birchbark cart.

The farmer had no horses to pull the cart, so the hedgehog boy ran after the two big squawking roosters in the chicken yard and snatched them up in his arms. Tethered to the cart, the roosters cackled and clawed at the ground.

The hedgehog boy jumped in and shouted good-by to his mother and father.

Away ran the roosters, crowing and flapping, with the cart jolting behind them on its wooden wheels.

By next morning, it was rumbling and bumping over the stony streets of the town.

What a sight! A boy like a hedgehog in a birchbark cart with roosters for horses!

Boys and girls stopped making wreaths for Midsummer Eve. Fathers dropped the wood they had been gathering for Midsummer bonfires. Mothers left their Midsummer baking. They all ran out of their houses to stare at the hedgehog boy.

In the town hall the fat prime minister leaned out the window and yelled at the children on the street, "Throw sticks at him! Throw stones!"

In the tavern the old general put down his mug of beer and shouted at his men, "Where are your spears, you fools?"

But the roosters cackled and flew up out of the way. Beating their wings and crowing, they came down safely in front of the castle.

There stood the king with his three daughters. Glumly, he welcomed the hedgehog boy. Then he turned to his youngest daughter and shuffled his feet. "Well, my dear," he said, "here is your husband."

The two older princesses laughed and teased their sister. "What a handsome husband!" jeered one. "How will you hug your prickly bridegroom?" giggled the other.

The youngest princess trembled. But then she remembered that the hedgehog boy had saved her life, and she held out her hand. "A promise is a promise," she said bravely.

The wedding bells were ringing in the steeple of the cathedral. The priest took his fine robes out of the closet.

In the castle the king sighed and looked for his best shirt. There was a hole in his sock. He couldn't find his gloves. Where had he put his amber crown?

The princess opened her bridal chest. Her finery was ready. She had made it all herself, and threaded a thousand beads into the stiff fabric of her headdress.

Was it for a hedgehog bridegroom that she had worked so hard?

In the cathedral the two older princesses waited beside their rich husbands, and snickered at their sister's bad luck. But the princess opened the church door and walked boldly to the altar, to take her place beside the hedgehog boy.

The king was late. At last, grumbling and muttering, he joined the wedding party, tripping over his shoes, which were too small and hurt his feet. The music struck up, and soon the wedding was over.

The priest cried, "And now you are husband and wife." The bells clashed in the steeple, and the roosters crowed in the street.

Once again the Midsummer bonfires were burning. Young men ran through the streets carrying torches. There was music and singing. The pigs squealed in the barnyard of the castle. The horses stamped in the stable.

ABOUT THE BOOK

Latvia, located in a northern corner of Europe on the edge of the Baltic Sea, was historically an agrarian culture. In ancient times the forces of nature—sun, moon, rain, wind—which so strongly affected the Latvians' daily lives, were perceived to be powerful deities. Gradually, each deity was identified by a particular symbol, which was, in turn, thought to have magical powers. While the meanings of these symbols were often lost or forgotten, the early forms, symmetrical and simple, have survived over the centuries in Latvian folk art.

In the earliest periods of Latvian design, red, yellow, blue, and green were the colors most frequently used. They were created from dyes made from natural sources such as blossoms, leaves, bark, and roots. Yellow was one of the most easily obtained colors, and it produced the widest range of shades, from pale yellow to dark ocher and brown.

The illustrations in this book, including the borders and costumes, reflect the distinctive traits of Latvian color and design that have survived the centuries and still constitute the essence of Latvian folk art. The folksong "Kur Tu Teci, Gailīti Manu" is an example of one of the sixty thousand dainas, songs that described daily life in ancient Latvia.

Text composed in Monotype Centaur by A. Colish, Inc., Mount Vernon, New York.

Color separations by Offset Separations Corp., New York, New York.

Printed by Rae Publishing Co., Inc., Cedar Grove, New Jersey

Design by Albert M. Cetta

Production by Miranda Book

1 8 1 7